T0067960

A Marine's
PEACE

ANDRES SANCHEZ

authorHOUSE®

AuthorHouse™
1663 Liberty Drive
Bloomington, IN 47403
www.authorhouse.com
Phone: 833-262-8899

Published by AuthorHouse   04/07/2022

ISBN: 978-1-6655-4551-8 (sc)
ISBN: 978-1-6655-4550-1 (e)

Library of Congress Control Number: 2021923958

Print information available on the last page.

CONTENTS

Preface..vii

Embassy Besieged.. 1
Shadows of Past 7
Fresh Start 27
Baseball Practice.. 31
Heat in Iraq 35
Last Goodbye 38
Anxious Moments.. 40
Unknown Journey.. 42
The Wait 47
The Ride Home.. 50
Collateral Damage... 53

Summary.. 59

PREFACE

The death of a family member is a difficult emotion to comprehend. You answer a late-night phone call from a relative and their soft, sad tone as they greet you establishes the mindset for the rest of the news. Crying ensues and the rest of the family wants to know what is being said. A pause in the conversation allows the message to be passed on and then the whole family begins to weep. Deep felt sobbing, uncontrollable anguish expressed as tears soak every available tissue. There is no easy answer to why the person was taken. You are never ready for the passing of a young person. Blame becomes paramount as you hear the circumstances and quickly find fault with everyone involved but realize that blaming others makes the loss more painful.

So, it was with my nephew John Sanchez, Jr. aka Johnny. A young Marine Corporal, with numerous medals for his service in Desert Storm. After his discharge from the Marines and several battles of civilian life, he settled and knew that he was on a good path for his family as expressed to his Aunt Maria. Johnny was a humble person with a distinguishable crackling nasal voice, loving and dedicated to his family. He had great compassion for others and cried when he would recount the battlefield experiences. I was familiar with some of his military adventures, trauma and some of the issues that triggered his PTSD, but his life had a purpose. We need to appreciate our time as a family and value our differences and challenges and support one another as we wait to meet our creator. I hope these few stories will inspire a more nurturing attitude towards our veterans, because they carry an indescribable hurt for which there is no cure.

EMBASSY BESIEGED

"SHOOT ANYONE THAT GETS THROUGH THE GATE," ordered the commanding officer. Johnny was startled with the command. He looked to the gate at the entrance of the embassy and noticed it being breached. His state of mind became overwhelmed, as he envisioned dead bodies throughout the embassy gate area. This order was unacceptable the murder of these people could not happen! Johnny shuffled over to the commander and requested to help with crowd control. The six- foot four, cigar chewing; John Wayne want-to-be officer sized-up Johnny with his eyes and with a smirk nodded his head in an acknowledgement of the request. He pulled the cigar out of his mouth and told Johnny that he had ten minutes to fix the problem. Johnny, a thin five-foot seven Marine Corporal took control.

"You!" Pointing at the Marines beside the commander, "come help push the crowd," Johnny's command directed at the guards near the entrance to the embassy. The whole group quickly turned to Commander Miller, and he swung his hand at them in acknowledgment of Johnny's order. Johnny took the lead and they followed him to the black ten-foot rod iron gate of the embassy. The troops moved close to the gate and the crowd retreated. This helped the process and quickly the Marines were in a pushing contest with the crowd. "Push! Ready, Push," yelled Johnny. Slowly the local Somali natives moved behind the iron gate. The black gate was tall and heavy, but these qualities appeared insignificant in comparison to the effort by the mass of scared, screaming people wanting in.

Another group of young militants from the community joined the battle to enter the embassy. Johnny ordered the incoming group to stay back, but they ignored or did not understand him. More Marines joined the pushing crusade, but the screaming, mad bunch of natives were succeeding. Johnny knew that failure was going to result in a tragic report about a massacre; for which he is now in command, therefore responsible. Failure was not an option. Looking for a solution, he noticed a piece of cable off to the side of the gate and away from the motorized pully. The thin eight-foot cable was interfering with the pushing contest. The Marines were stepping on it and kicked it out of the way. It tumbled to his feet.

That was the answer. Slowly bending over, Johnny grabbed the cable with his right hand, wrapped it around his wrist and secured it to his hand. His eyes scanned the situation, and yelled at the top of his lungs, "move back!" Again, and again, but little progress in five minutes. Johnny's grip tightened on the eight-foot cable as it dragged behind him and his left-hand waving at the crowd to move back. Each step towards the screaming, angry mob became more dreadful, he was unsure if they were carrying weapons, but just in case, he yelled at four Marines behind him to stand ready with their weapons. Johnny hated this situation; his skirmishes in Desert Storm as a point man was to take enemy fire and again, he could not see the enemy, but this time his Marine brothers had rifles set on potential targets. He began his crusade, yelling and encouraging the other Marines to push the crowd back and close the gate. Three attempts at closing the gate had made little progress. Success was dismal. Marines were slowly being pushed back, but the commanding officer barked out orders to shoot those trespassing on to embassy grounds. Tension was high, as other Marines prepared their CAR-15's, Johnny mentally prayed for strength and forgiveness for what he was about to do. A cold sweat ran down the side of his face as the metallic snap of the rifles signaled the end of the incursion. Johnny pushed the other soldiers aside and prepared the crowd for the onslaught, the cable was firmly set on his right hand. Once more, Johnny yelled at the crowd to move back. The intruders up front stepped back in terror after they noticed the cable in hand, but not fast enough.

Johnny's right-hand reared back, as if to throw a

baseball, his left arm waving at the cluster of rebels urging them to move back, but they did not react promptly. No time to second guess the commander's action. "Move back, move back!" screaming and waving his arm, then a loud slapping sound was heard, and everyone froze. A young Somalian jumped back holding his shoulder and expressing flowery vocabulary as the metal cable slashed his shoulders several times. Eyes squinted; mouth gaping, heavy breathing as the iron whip continued its thrashing side to side, blood bursting from shoulders, hands, arms, and legs. There was no time to be diplomatic as far as Johnny was concerned. Other members of the rebel crowd began to move forward, but suddenly felt the sting of the iron whip. Single-handedly, swinging the cable from side to side, screaming and waving the people to get back and away. Suddenly, panic surged through the crowd as the Somalis jumped back in agony.

"What did I do?" no regret for what he had done, but hoping to have saved lives, as his eyes scanned the bloody iron whip. His adrenaline was out of control. The gate shut, the crowd retreated, but the excitement did not subside. It was not anger that drove his action, but fear for their safety. He swung the cable three more times at hands that gripped the iron gates. The hands swiftly moved away. His sense of anxiety decreased. He could see the crowd had stepped away fearful and bewildered.

This "crazy soldier, mad man, move away," bellowed

from the mouths of the trespassers. They had never experienced such fierce determination. Frightful, was the appearance of this lone Marine; eyes blaring, face dripping with sweat, arms partly curled hanging to his side, right hand gripping a cable dripping with blood. His shoulders looked broad, arms and clothes splattered with fresh blood. Goliath, no less, at that moment in time from the perspective of the unwitting spectators. It was not Goliath that Johnny favored, but David. He stood ready to strike the beast that was nurturing hysteria in the mass of people. You will not come in, Johnny thought. You will not come in! Johnny began reciting this melody. He stood ready with great conviction, reciting these words repeatedly.

His eyes scanned the crowd. A gaze piercing their thoughts of rushing in. No one dared challenge this immense force. The rebel militant group stepped back, and their fear grew as four armed Marines, ready to shoot, walked and stood beside Johnny. "Good work Corporal," whispered Commander Harris, as he softly touched Johnny's left shoulder.

Johnny's legs wanted to buckle. His heart was beating out of his chest. The veins on his forearms swelled like a weightlifter on steroids. Johnny moved back; other troops secured the area, then he did an about-face as tears dripped from his eyes. Now he was angry, or was he afraid? A deep breath cleared his anxiety. His mind confused. Death was not new to him as he continued walking. His eyes fixed on the mass of people staring, bewildered by his rage. At this point he knew he would not have nightmares. These faces would disappear and never bother him again.

"Hey Johnny, are you OK?" His uncle Toby, a former US Air Force personnel, slapped his behind. Johnny snapped out of his daze and looked at his uncle with his usual smile then his nasal crackled voice responding, "hi Tío, thanks for the wake-up call." Johnny was witty, but the slap from his uncle caught him off guard. Conversation with his uncle was usually a lost battle. However, this time he was thankful for being removed from his walking nightmare. Toby chuckled and walked away after he gave Johnny a squeeze with his right arm demonstrating his superior strength.

SHADOWS OF PAST

THE LONG STRETCH OF LAND BETWEEN THE BEGINNING of the row of plum trees and the end was a mental quest for Johnny. Each time a piston ignited in the red beast, memories of death and destruction came rushing at him. Never a moments rest as the limbs from the plum trees caused him to lean or duck as if in battle. Desperately, he would slap himself in attempt to keep awake while driving the tractor, but that was a temporary distraction of the memories he confronted. No one knew about the shadows that haunted his soul. As his mind lingered in self-pity a low thin limb gently touched his shoulder and forced attention to the slow steady speed of the tractor. Johnny reached and moved the limb away from his arm. A small spur on the limb managed to scrape across his palm, causing a small cut.

A trickle of blood appeared below the lower part of his pinky. Johnny tried to ignore this minor cut, but his memories dominated his mental state. The site of blood sparked the helicopter conflict in Somalia. His hand cut by a piece of metal as he lifted a solider from the helicopter wreckage. Screaming, crying, people yelling; "shoot them," arms tired, thirsty, but determined to save his fellow Marines. Johnny swinging his rifle from side to side, threatening anyone trying to move towards them. Finally, help from another platoon waiting for them at the end of the village. The smell of ripe fruit and stifling air was relentless in the recall of so much tragedy.

Johnny's mind had left him for just a second, then a rush of anger made him react. He lifted his left foot and pushed the clutch as his right hand deaccelerated the throttle lever by the steering wheel. The tractor came to an abrupt stop. The heavy hydraulic disks prevented any movement once the clutch was applied. His right hand released the accelerator lever and reached to set the transmission lever into neutral. The loud piston noise was now a low thump-thump-thump, echoing the beat of his busy heart. Johnny paused and caught his breath, looked behind him and was able to catch a glimpse of his son hunting the black birds feasting on worms.

Johnny reached with his left hand and turned the key to quiet the engine, it jumped and coughed a few times then it went silent. His eyes began to strain, he searched for the little limb that caused him all this mental furry. As he shifted his head to the direction of the limb; his mind collapsed back to a time he wished had never happened. The smell of diesel, dirt and the sight of blood revived his sense of combat. He looked at the front of the tractor and envisioned the front of the camouflaged Humvee. "Solider take cover behind the door, watch the window on the second floor there's movement," Johnny yelled at the nineteen-year-old Marine.

He was careful, for there was no telling from which direction a sniper bullet would hit you. The Humvee did not move, his gaze became fixed on the shadows moving by the window. Several of his friends had fallen prey to carelessness and he was determined not to lose another. Once again, the image passed by the window. Johnny quickly moved into the building to his left. He ordered the Humvee driver to pull back for surveillance of the building to the right. The driver acknowledged with a thumbs-up signal. The engine started, wheels reversed and moved inches away from the building to the right. Johnny looked at the troops in the Humvee and with his right hand commanded two of them to the building to the right and three to his side of the street. No doubting his commands, no questions; Johnny, the Corporal, was in command. They switched their headphones on and listened to execute their next order.

"Augie, Tom, go to the roof and report what you see, over;" commanded Johnny. Both snipers snapped their rifles onto their shoulders and quickly reached the top. Johnny and the three other troops maneuvered themselves in and out of doorways and shadows until they reached a clean line of sight to the entry of the building under surveillance. All the men waited anxiously for some intel from the troops at the roof top. Three, four, five minutes passed and no communication. Then, a whispering voice, "Commander, a small contingency of men, between three to five are preparing some explosives; over," whispered Augie. "Sir, two have press passes around their necks-over," continued Augie. "Verify authentic-passes-over," Johnny hoping they were not real. "Press pass confirmed, clear as day, with big letters," Augie's voice became excited. A whistle, then loud cheering; "Augie have you been spotted?" inquired Johnny. "No sir," silence for a few seconds, but those few seconds without a word were a sign of danger, then Augie noted, "movement, second floor, body vests being strapped, total five men-over." Johnny had a bad feeling. If the press passes were real, he would be in real trouble, but why were they involved? His doubt caused him to take more time than usual to respond. "Sir, orders-over," requested Augie. "No one leaves the building-over," commanded Johnny. "Yes sir- out," replied Augie.

Johnny was keenly aware that he had been noticed by the locals, but not the rest of his troops. Augie and Tom were very crafty and invisible when they were on task. Shuffling feet in the house was signaling panic, but Johnny did not want them to become aware of the troops on the roof. Johnny was worried about his command to shoot the reporters and began to doubt his order. "Sir, the two with passes have moved behind the wall," cautioned Augie. "Are any strapped?" asked Johnny. "No reporter is strapped, but one other civilian is and a second is being prepared-over," responded Augie. "I'll wait for your order Sir, target is fixed-over," Augie responded. "Are the reporters US-over," inquired Johnny. "Sir, they do not appear to be US-over," Augie expected to hear his last command.

Johnny was completely confused and felt worried about his next order. "Augie are the civilians friendly? -over," asked Johnny. "No sir-over," with an extra emphasis on no by Augie. These were not the words Augie expected or wanted to hear. Augie believed his commander was having second thoughts. Augie was sure that they and the other troops would become the victims of this plot. Augie had decided to protect his commander, without his blessing. He could see the path right to the commander from the building they were targeting. There was no time to waste, waiting for orders. Augie set his target, while Tom plotted and marked the other targets. He was ready, finger on trigger. Augie took a deep breath, but Tom touched his shoulder and shook his head, making sure that Augie did not fire. Tom was aware of the tension, but he was there to make sure that all orders were obeyed. The shadows were gathering by the front door of the building, then a soft voice, but a clear command came through. "No one walks out-over," directed Johnny. Tom and Augie locked eyes and thumbs up by Tom; Augie was cleared to follow his orders.

No sooner had Johnny given the command when a burst of gun fire echoed on the walls of the buildings. Several loud explosions flushed the air and shocked the Humvee that protected the troops on the ground. Pieces of stone flew onto the street as the two troops with Johnny positioned themselves for enemy fire. One crouched low and the other aimed higher. "Three down, second floor, two reporters unable to confirm-over," said Augie. "Keep your sight on the door and," before Johnny could finish his command, he heard a calling out, "Press," yelled out a robed person. Too late to change his mind. Six rounds of rapid fire silenced the entire neighborhood. It was quiet for several minutes; the only noise was the shuffling feet in the sand. Out of the shadows and crevices of the buildings; women draped from head to toe, cautiously entered the streets, not knowing who was laying on the ground. Was it their brother, father or son lying dead in the hot Somalian dirt? They would soon discover their identities. Suddenly, a loud vibrating yell, raised the hair on the back of the soldier's necks. That signaled the death of a relative. The yelling changed to a high pitch cry that scorched the souls of all within hearing distance.

"Sir, all targets are down, over." "Augie, the two reporters?" before Johnny could finish his request, Augie began the response; with soft repenting words, "they're down – over." Johnny took a deep breath and began to playout the next set of procedures and consequences. "What did I do," he thought with a sense of defeat, as two soldiers with bloodshot eyes wanting to see the fallen enemy, gave him shade. Johnny raised his eyes and fixed his gaze and with an inconsequential voice said, "dope heads, do not shoot the press! Get the bodies back to base and we will deal with it there," commanded Johnny.

Hours and hours of training to make sure the correct response would be used in combat; did he make a mistake? Johnny thought to himself. His self-confidence took over as he assessed his gut feelings. "Augie are we clear, over?" requested Johnny. "Clear to approach, over," responded Augie. Johnny slipped out from behind the door and ordered the two troops to secure the area. They quickly moved into the house and confirmed the death of the Somalian militants. Each step that Johnny took enhanced the nightmare scenario. Visions flashed before him as tracer bullets chase enemy fire, but the bullets chased him. How to dodge this nightmare was the next battle. Each action endeared a greater sense of depression. His career was no more. Illusions of being this great hero Marine shattered into tiny irretrievable pieces.

Augie did not care about being humble. He walked, making as much noise as possible, letting every person know that he was responsible for the five bodies lying lifeless in the house. Johnny turned and killed Augie's boasting attitude with his piercing gaze. "This is not a celebration", stated Johnny. Justin: A First lieutenant, anticipated the need for assistance and his group arrived just as the crowd began to chant, "Yankees out, Yankees out." Quickly, the First Lieutenant had the area secured and the bodies bagged. Justin walked to Johnny and said, "Oh shit! Did you not see the press pass?" "Yes," with a confidence that made Justin step back. "Ok, don't talk until the debriefing, got it?" "Yes Sir!" Johnny responded without wavering his sense of conviction because he knew his was right.

Tom and Augie followed and assured Johnny that no mistake occurred. "Hey, you did the right thing, they were waist deep in their shit with the Taliban, don't worry." How was he not to worry, he had just received a NJP, Non -Judicial Punishment for whipping civilians, but this was a Summary Court-Martial matter, which is a more serious matter. His Commanding officer's report availed him with a dismissal for the earlier offense, however this time he did not save lives, instead he took five and two of those are thought to be U. S. news reporters. Johnny jumped into the Humvee and did not say a single word to the others for the entire trip back to the base. The other Marines did not bother Johnny, because they knew that Johnny's future as a Marine depended upon the consistency in the debriefing. The silence was disturbing for all in the

Humvee. Michael: a muscular five foot-five, Marine from San Diego, sat crouched on the floor facing Johnny, he looked up as if to ask a question, but reconsidered when he assessed the profound, contemplative stare on Johnny's face. A sudden stop on the six-kilometer trek to the base stirred everyone to action. The silent journey quickly changed into a search mission for IED's. Augie sat in the front seat and noticed recent diggings by the roadside. This prompted the team to form a search grid for possible IED's, fortunately no IED's after twenty minutes, and they were on the Humvee and back to the base camp.

The drive had now become long, the sun was delivering waves of heat over one-hundred ten degrees Fahrenheit, and no air conditioning. The heat, silence, slow maneuvering to avoid any potential IED's was increasing the anticipated anguish of potential consequences. A large bump on the road triggered everyone's reaction, instantly hands clasped their weapons, bodies readied to exit the Humvee; "It's just a big rock," Augie stated. "Gentlemen, this is not the time to be daydreaming, no-one saw the rock?" "It could have been our last trip I don't want to go home in a body bag, Wake Up!" Johnny's loud voice intended for himself as well because he was indulging in self-pity until the bump on the road. The fighting fuse extinguished. "The party is over boys," Augie teased. His antics were not appreciated at times, but today it started an uncontrollable laughter that did not stop until they neared the entry of the base.

Beach front property that looked more like a junk yard than a Marine base, except for the helicopters non-stop landing and departure from the area. The walls were two high stacked metal containers. Johnny felt every turn as the vehicle's brakes tightened, the brake pads squealed like a dying pig. Maneuvering between the opening of the metallic wall, the vehicle headed straight to the Commanding Officers building. His jeep parked near the entry, which indicated he had been driven to the site. The Humvee's tires skidded to a stop behind another armored vehicle near the entry, the door opened, a few chuckles were still reminiscing the tension of the earlier experience. The troops exited the vehicle and walked over to a small debriefing room. Johnny looked up at the extended white container structure to both sides of the commander's office. Johnny's knees felt weak, stomach had an empty sensation, as he contemplated scenarios of his next few days and weeks. He took a deep breath hoping to relax and his appearance would be of a calm, collective, confident person. He knew the orders were justified, enemies disguised with friendly signs, they would not hesitate to take the troop's lives.

He had no doubt they were directly involved in suicide bombings in and around Mogadishu. To make matters worse, some of these self-proclaimed martyrs were employed by media companies; who had access to our information and resources. It now became clear to Johnny, why troops were killed despite the effort the commanders took to keep the troop's whereabouts secret. Johnny delved into various failed missions and embraced the conclusion that mission information had been breached. How? He whispered to himself. He thought for a few moments about recent events and knew his gut feeling to be true. Missions in Hiran, Marka were a disaster.

He recalled a reconnaissance mission to Marka; beautiful seaside city, devastated by war about fifty miles from the base, where a young American; laid in the hot dirty street taking his last breath; eyes darkened, skin paled as blood stopped flowing, this image was the result of the information breach. He took a platoon on reconnaissance; to what they thought was a peaceful resort, then several shots were heard. One of the leading troops screamed, "I'm hit!" Johnny's fragile one-hundred-fifty-pound body stumbled thirty yards before reaching the young Marine. The other troops returned fire; they shattered every wall of the building within rifle range of the enemy. Shells littered the streets, crying, screaming, pleas of mercy heard over the muffled impact of the bullets, ripping the buildings apart. Johnny raised his clenched fist, and all went silent. The troops eager for more; as they reloaded, but no shuffling of feet, crying, setting a bullet in a chamber; hearts beating furiously ready for another barrage, but silence was now the element of surprise. No mourning or loud chattering when women see their dead family members. Johnny cautiously walked the last few steps to the fallen Marine. Every step Johnny took encountered a hopeless feeling. The Marine had dropped his equipment as he stumbled to the ground. Johnny removed the Marine's vest and placed a wad of gauze on the wound just below his left arm pit.

A small hole was on the under shirt of the Marine's vest, then the chest cavity gently moved. Hope suddenly reappeared. Quickly, a medic's hand reached to the body, gauze covered the wound, words of encouragement uttered, but not heard. The chest moved once, twice, then no more. This young man's first assignment as a point man had proven to be his last. Johnny's conviction of being right was now transforming into defiance. "Sir, please!" a voice jarred him from his memory, an MP assigned to Johnny was now escorting him to a detention area.

The Humvee was at a stop. Commander Miller's voice ordered the driver to step aside as the MP's walked to the back of the vehicle. Johnny's routine was a brief ceremony congratulating him on the success of his missions, but he was now being escorted to detention by his friends. "Hey, we're just doing our job," said a young MP. They had no desire to escalate the tension, the arrest was difficult enough. The MP's knew Johnny and felt they were betraying him as they continually apologized for placing him in handcuffs. As the cuffs were being placed; an oil slick caused Johnny to slip and fall. The MP's jerked apprehensively, as they were caught off guard. "Relax, at ease fellows," Johnny blurted some reassuring words to the MP's. Their tension was on high alert, which at times provoked unwanted reactions, but that was not the situation with Johnny. Slowly he balanced himself, brought his gaze to meet each of the MP's eyes, and without a word said, they all completed their work without acknowledgement, that his detention was wrong, as they followed orders.

The tall thin MP broke the silence, by ordering Johnny to the Commander's office. Each footstep on the dirt and gravel road echoed against the white walls of the Commander's office. The MP stretched his long arm towards Johnny to open the entry door to the command center. Johnny could sense the emotions from his team, but the team was not to intervene with the case at hand. This was no longer a Non-Judicial Proceeding, but a Court Martial for the death of two reporters. Johnny was sure he gave the right order and was convinced he would beat the allegations. Johnny was within months of leaving the service and he was considering reenlisting, but this situation had placed him in an entirely different mindset.

"How could this be happening to me," he mumbled to himself, which made the MP turn his head. "Sir," the MP suggested, "can I help you with something?"

"No," with a straight stare into the MP's eyes, "I am just thinking out loud." The MP turned his head with a slight tilt as if questioning Johnny's state of mind. Stepping simultaneously with the MP, Johnny entered the Commander's office, took several steps into the room, then froze.

It was not fear, nor training, but a sense of betrayal that surpassed his respect for the commander. Slowly Johnny took two steps toward the large mahogany desk. The room was empty, but he set his left foot firmly onto the floor, then brought his right boot and slapped his feet together and stood at attention. His arms clasped by handcuffs at his lower back with chest and shoulders affixed in a stiff posture. The stench of cigar was as suffocating as the arrogance of Commander Miller. The Commander's cigar stench was here, but he was not. Several minutes passed, which gave Johnny time to conduct mental deliberations about the situation, but each scenario ended in conflict. Johnny's imagination was beyond control. Yelling his rationale about the mission, swearing at anyone near him, fighting, kicking, hitting—no easy solution to his convoluted thoughts. It was not the Commander's, MPs, or his troops he was having imaginary conflicts with, but his subconscious. Uneasy with his distorted thoughts, Johnny shook his head and grounded himself with reality.

The cigar stench and the unconventional executive leather chair did not match the desert battle scene, but it did give the Commander an aura of authority, for which contempt spued with every breath exhaled, but he knew to keep that to himself, even though the Commander did order his detention. A tall thin MP broke the ice, by requesting Johnny take a chair on the left side of the desk. Johnny thought, "why the left side, when I can sit in front of the desk," the MP; stiff as a board, definitively pointed to the chair on the left side of the desk. Johnny decided that this was not the time to be overconfident, because the Commander was an extremely strict, 'rule of law,' person and this battle was not worth fighting. He proceeded to the left and noticed a picture of President Bush, hung on the right side, behind the desk. Johnny sat quietly, recalling an incident in school when he sat in the office of the school Principal, for punching another student. As his memory stirred the past, noise echoed from the outside behind the door. Footsteps, though faint, but certainly coming to the door. Johnny's face broke into a cold sweat. The steps stopped. His eyes focused on the doorknob. Waiting, watching- no movement of the knob, the footsteps did not continue. Johnny knew the Commander was a few feet from him but would not enter. Johnny's face was dripping with dirt filled sweat drops. His hands handcuffed behind him therefore unable to clean his face, so he swiped his face on his shoulder which prompted the MP to turn and stare at him.

The doorknob made a slight clasping sound, then a

stream of stifling air rushed into the room. Johnny stood up and at attention, but his hands handcuffed and unable to salute his Commander. The Commander immediately ordered to remove his handcuffs, which the MP did. In a loud raspy voice from the Commander, "take a seat," "yes sir," Johnny replied and sat. The Commander had a file with Johnny's name and picture on it, which the Commander had not read. The Commander continued to labor over several pages, then said, "I'm going to ask one simple question before we start." "Yes sir, what is your question?" replied Johnny in a crisp, but not challenging voice. The Commander asked, "Why are you here?" "Sir I am in the dark with this situation, because we completed the mission you assigned us." Replied Johnny. "I want to know what you did. Not about the orders," barked out the Commander. Johnny in a slow but confident voice replied, "at approximately 15:30 hours, I ordered our troops to open fire on enemy Combatants, and they did." "They took down all those identified as responsible for the killing of some of our troops," responded Johnny. The Commander took a deep breath, attempting to keep calm. He took another deep breath, turned to Johnny then said, "did you notice that two of the men had large press passes?"

Johnny's voice was definitely stern. "Yes Sir, we knew." "Then why the hell did you order to take them down?" asked the Commander. "Sir, we had good intel on those two. They were solely responsible for the deaths of several troops," Johnny responded, voice filled with conviction. "We had them under surveillance for several days and tracked them to several sites where IED's were being made," responded Johnny. The Commander listened carefully and paged through several pages of briefing and intel reports. The Commander postured hesitantly, "you better hope your evidence holds up, you're not under arrest, but I want you to stay in your tent until you are ordered otherwise, understood?" before the Commander could look away Johnny said, "No sir." With his cigar now in hand, the Commander's raspy voice demanded, "what do you mean 'no sir,' what don't you understand?"

Johnny's stress was in red alert, "no sir, I understand, but I'm either detained or not." "I did nothing wrong, retrieve the bodies, finish the investigation before you decide to place me in detention," demanded Johnny.

The Commander was not expecting any defiance, which made him choose his next words carefully. "You are not here to determine the outcome of this investigation, nor are you here to be barking orders at me, do you hear me?" Johnny humbly looked down and said, "yes sir, may I speak freely?" "You are speaking freely," said the Commander. "No sir, because this just happened and I'm being tried and the investigation has not been conducted," even though Johnny's face was calm it had changed color and was perspiring again. Johnny's mouth became dry.

His stress became anger as the Commander continued to recite the names of the media companies that claimed their reporters were murdered. Johnny had tuned out the Commander, then looked straight into the Commander's eyes with a clear intent to challenge his authority. This defiance made the Commander bark an order to the MP to place Johnny in the brig. Just as the MP moved toward Johnny, the Commander lifted his hand to stop. He took a deep breath and decided to react with calmness. Johnny however was determined to win this non-verbal argument. Johnny's tension was at a point that consequences did not matter, he was done being humble.

The Commander realized that Johnny was not about to give up and sit in his tent and unless he charged him with a crime, he could not place him in the brig. The Commander pleaded that he was getting hammered about the two reporters. The Commander wanted assurance that his orders had been followed. With a reassuring voice Johnny satisfied that inquiry. "Call the media companies, ask them if they are missing two reporters, because the targets were not reporters, two days ago they were unemployed." Johnny's voice was assertive but inspired with contempt for those that placed him in this situation. The Commander chuckled at the thought of calling because he imagined the reply, "yes, the two you killed were foreign reporters," he thought would be the response. "You know Johnny, that's not a bad idea, I'm going to ask the admiral and let us wait for an answer. However, you need to stay confined until notified."

With a glance by the Commander at the MP, standing stiff as a board by the door, both individuals accepted the situation and the MP escorted Johnny to his detention tent. As they walked to his tent, Johnny looked at the Marine Sargeant in his khaki shirt, blue pants, and his name tag above his right pocket. His last name was Ramirez, so Johnny thought he would tease him and asked, "what part of Mexico are you from Ramirez?" The six-foot two MP looked straight into Johnny's eyes and said, "I'm from East LA, I'm not Mexican." They walked out of the compound and around the back where the long-covered tent sat behind the ten-foot-high fence with razor wire at the top. Ramirez asked Johnny to stop, as the other MP on the inside of the school type gate, pulled out his key for the lock, opened it, and motioned to enter.

Johnny was directed to a table where a baby-faced MP; Berg, in his makeshift booking office, would complete his entry in the detention tent. After taking his information, Ramirez escorted Johnny through pale green flaps that opened into a ten by ten completely wired enclosure. There was another ten-foot razor wired enclosure in the perimeter of this one. There was only one door in the back and one at the front. Sleeping cots were on both sides of the room, but there was no one else in sight. The door lock could be heard from where he was standing, and

Ramirez returned to his post at the Commander's office. The booking officer yelled out to Johnny, "take a break sir, Commander Miller is working on your case, you'll be out in no time." "I sure hope so, because I was following his orders," replied Johnny with a tired voice. Johnny looked about and took several blankets from the other cots and sat on what he considered the most comfortable one. He was alone and thought he would be reprimanded for taking blankets from the other cots, but who cared if he took the blankets, it made it soft for him to lay down. The sun had settled behind the metal walls of the compound, bright orange plumes transformed the evening sky in Mogadishu. Johnny could hear the crashing of the waves from his beachside detention resort. He took deep breaths as he removed his boots, then laid face up on the cot and longed for being on his farm.

FRESH START

FARM LIFE IS CERTAINLY NOT EASY, BUT FOR JOHNNY IT was a fresh start. Even though he was born and raised a farmer, but now in his new journey, each step onto the land, was pleasurable. Instinctively, he treasured his life growing up on this same farm and now appreciated the experience of living off of the farm and the investment of life on the land. It was so different. His life's struggles had changed and for the better, now that he had full custody of his son, Isaac, and working for himself was a new beginning. He had the full support of all his farming family members, which were all around these communities, and he knew he could rely on them no matter the circumstances. This morning felt special. The air was fresh, and the plum orchard needed disking.

Johnny stepped out from the back porch of the farmhouse. He looked to his right and noticed a cat near the entry of the basement. It was a beautiful black and white cat, which kept the farmyard clean of mice. The cat's tail was shivering as it was set to pounce on something. Johnny froze. A moment he could not miss. Unable to see the side of the house; where the probable victim was hiding, he decided to wait until the cat would react. Hoping it would not be too long, because he needed to tend to the Queen Rosa plum orchard. He missed it. That thought made him look at the orchard and the cat had his pray in its mouth by the time he refocused on the event. Poor mouse. It wiggled for just a second, before this large cat began to devour it. He Slipped on his work shoes and headed for his mother's house, where he would have coffee and breakfast with his parents. Isaac was always at his grandparent's house before Johnny.

His walk across the dirt driveway felt different. The small garage to his right was leaning and appeared ready to fall, but it has been that way since he could remember. His father mentioned that an old barn was behind the garage, and it fell, because it leaned like that for years. The cool air in the early morning was pleasant. The smell of coffee welcomed his sense of satisfaction as he stepped into his parent's house. Their house was thirty yards away and it also had a back porch, which allowed access straight into the kitchen. Johnny entered, gave his mother a hug and she quickly ordered him to sit and have breakfast with the rest of the family.

There was nothing better than, a fresh cup of Folgers coffee and a morning meeting with his Dad to discuss politics and the day's chores. He carefully sat and greeted his Father and began to sip his coffee. "Mijo, are you going to disk the plums?" asked his Father. "Yes, after breakfast, because I have practice with my championship team at three," responded Johnny. "Do you need any help," asked Dad. "No, if I don't finish today, I'll finish tomorrow," "thanks Dad." Johnny had a relentless work ethic, and he knew he could finish the ten acres before two, but just in case he didn't, he decided to give himself an extra day.

Work around the farm never ends. Today is disking, tomorrow is watering and the next day is? who knows what? That is farm life. Constant busy work to develop your new crop and make enough money for the year and for your livelihood. Johnny finished his breakfast and asked Isaac to be ready to leave by two for his baseball practice. He kissed his son and told him to behave while he worked. Unbeknownst to Johnny, Isaac had made his own plans for the day. He had readied his pellet rifle to hunt birds that day. He would let his Dad disk a few rows in the plum orchard then hunt the birds that feed on the exposed worms. Isaac enjoyed this hunting adventure; Johnny knew and was constantly on the lookout for his son while on the tractor.

Johnny thanked his mother, gave her a kiss, and walked out the back door to the tractor behind the lean-to tool shed. The red Massey Ferguson tractor was older than Johnny, but it was reliable and ready with the hydraulic disks. Johnny chuckled, because his Dad left it ready for him. He saddled the old seat, which was covered with an old cushion, grabbed the steering wheel, set his fingers on the ignition key, and let the tractor roar. This gorgeous red beast had been here since the beginning of this farm, and it jumped as each piston moved up and down. Johnny pushed the accelerator lever just a little to stabilize the acceleration of the red beast and sure as the yellow of gold, its pistons settled and purred like a hungry lion. Johnny reached over to the hydraulic lever and lifted the disk apparatus. Disks up, he was set and ready to drive the tractor to the Queen Rosa plum orchard, where he was to disk the weeds between the trees, then he glanced to his right for a brief second and noticed a young man in camouflage pants walking into the orchard thirty yards away. He knew Isaac had been waiting for this moment to hunt with his new pellet rifle. Well, he better start the work so they could both get the day's chores done before baseball practice.

BASEBALL PRACTICE

LATE EVENING, THE LAST PRACTICE FLYBALL CAUGHT BY David, then all the players are called into the dugout. Parents waited patiently for practice to end. Johnny signaled for the catcher to pick up the equipment. The team was doing great. They were the team to beat. Good pitchers, hitters and just a great well-rounded group of 10-year-old boys. Johnny looked out to right field and waved his hand for the players to run in. Suddenly a shiver throughout his body made him cringe.

His jaws tightened. The muscles on his cheeks quivered. The cold chill was accompanied by screaming voices filled with terror. "I'm shot! Help me. Get Me Out. Johnny! get me out!" the screaming agony echoing unwanted memories. His Marine brothers, their voices faded with the blistering heat wave of the San Joaquin Valley. The smell of gun powder, bullets whistling near him, sand in his eyes, haunting memories he dreaded, so difficult to dismiss and to think of them only as a dream.

"Dad! let's go," his son's voice made his thoughts

regain reality. The heat was not much different, late afternoon and close to one hundred degrees, as his eyes looked up to the sky. Enjoying the screams that came from his baseball team and his son's friends. Quietly, he thanked God, acknowledged his son's calling to leave the field and go home. Johnny nodded and waved his hand to concede to his son's demands. His thoughts, however lingered at the forefront of his emotions.

There was no getting out of this dilemma. At least not right away. He had been home for eight years and his life had been in disarray, but at present it was much better. With full custody of Isaac, his own home and most important working on the farm with his father. He had a euphoric feeling. He was at the right place. His life made sense. The warm summer heat was comforting. A gentle satisfaction he could not express. With his arm on his son's shoulder they walked behind David, who would ride with them after practice.

David was their best pitcher and his son's best friend. Johnny would never hesitate to bring him to practice or take him home. Seeing his son with a friend that shared jokes and made trivial talk about other teams and players, reinforced his conviction that his choice of leaving the military was correct.

"Race you to the car," "ok," they acknowledged the desire to compete. The race was on. The two thoroughbred ten-year-old boys were off. Their legs fanned the heat waves of the San Joaquin Valley as they raced to the edge of the backstop fence. They turned the corner neck and neck, took deep breaths as they hurled their legs forward and turned their bodies to the pickup. Cleats thrashing the grass on each step, dust began to fly as they entered the dirt parking lot area. Best friends, but no mercy for each other, jockeying for position to the vehicle. Closer and closer to the truck no clear leader as they both reached out to touch the back. "I won," "I won," both extended their arms and did their victory dance. All this excitement reminded Johnny of so many similar scrimmages with his cousins. Other memories started to engage his mind and merge with the present. Each step, in one-hundred-degree heat, sparked a jolt of his dreadful war experiences. Johnny was an exceptional runner, which qualified him to become a point man for the Marines.

The heat, dust, his boys yelling and bouncing about turned his mind from the present to the past. He could now taste the sand from his Desert Storm combat. He continued to stroll to his truck and each step reminding him of different events. Falling upon the sand, bullets whistling as they missed him. Returned fire by his troops; would silence the opposition, but only for a moment. A huge breath of hot dry air prepared his lungs for another ten to twenty-yard sprint. Troops focused on keeping their point man safe. He raised his hand slightly and his troops knew that within a five second count, he would sprint again. It was their job to neutralize the enemy fire without getting him killed. "Hurry up Dad," Isaac's voice shook his senses back to Reedley, California.

It was like falling from the Sky, then blasted with a giant air blower as he realized he was pulling his keys from his pocket. "Jump in boys," Johnny ordered as the two wrestled with each other, trying to gain shotgun position. Johnny could not help but laugh. What a wonderful day, his son enjoying himself, experiencing things in life that would give him a sound basis to harness lifelong friendship. "Boys let's go," ordered Johnny.

HEAT IN IRAQ

ISAAC AND DAVID QUICKLY JUMPED IN THE CABIN OF THE small truck and instantly cried out for the air conditioner. It was hot! The truck windows were closed thereby making the charcoal gray interior much hotter. It was an oven and the boys complained about the two-hundred-degree heat. Then in a slow compassionate voice Johnny began talking to the boys about the heat in Somalia and Iraq. The boys new the routine. Isaac nudged David on the ribs and gestured with his eyebrows and a head movement for David to start the heat in Iraq routine.

"Coach how hot was Iraq?" David giggled, as they all knew the first answer. Johnny started with his usual, "it was so hot," then the boys simultaneously interrupted and in choir finished, "that you could cook eggs on the clip of your rifle." Johnny smiled and continued with the routine. "It was so hot," boys properly bated, "that you could bathe with your own sweat." "It was so hot, that buzzards would fall from the sky barbequed," finished the boys. This routine continued until they reached the

Englehart ranch. Isaac jumped out of the truck, quickly punched David on the arm and said, "you're it," then ran to his grandparent's home. David was caught off guard and unable to punch back, instead he waved and said, "bye."

Johnny knew that his parents would have dinner ready for his son. Isaac's Grandfather stepped out from behind the screen door and called out, "ándale Mijo." Johnny was not sure to whom that order was directed. However, he knew that they would provide for Issac. Isaac enjoyed going to his grandparent's house, because it was like walking into a museum and his father was the main attraction. "Isaac, where is your Dad going," asked Grandpa. "He's going to drop off David by Tía Maria's ranch, that's where David lives," responded Isaac. "He'll be home soon," added Isaac. Grandpa shook his head up and down, then put his arm around Isaac's shoulder and they both walked up the stairs, through the screen door and into the house.

Isaac could not wait to eat Grandma's food. Freshly made flour tortillas, which made the meal extra delicious. Grandpa showed Isaac the secret to eating flour tortillas. "While grandma's back is turned, you grab the butter knife, spread butter on the tortilla, roll it up, before Grandma finishes the rolling of a new tortilla". Grandpa and Isaac had this play down to a science. Of course, Grandma could see their mischievousness on the reflection of the kitchen window, but she enjoyed playing along with the boys. "What happened to all the butter?" she pretended not to know. Grandpa and Isaac would glare at each other and pretend not to understand what she was asking. The boys were sitting together, like usual, then Grandpa asked Isaac about baseball practice. Grandpa praised Isaac about being a better player than his uncle Ray. Just then, Grandma placed two bowls filled with pork, mole with rice, and a dozen tortillas. Isaac reached for the first tortilla but was told to wait until Grandma said 'Grace'. No sooner did she say 'Amen,' that Isaac reached, pulled the top tortilla, and began his ritual of butter and rolling it. Isaac forgot about Grandpa. He was too eager to start chewing the tasty pork and mole mouthful. He chewed away and had to stop to clean the dripping mole from the side of his mouth and clean his stained mole hands. Jaws wide open ready for another mouthful, suddenly Isaac froze.

A strange look on Isaac's face scared Grandpa, who was ready to crack a joke about Isaac's eating fury but decided to ask him if he was ok, instead. Isaac looked at his Grandpa with a sense of anticipation, ready to speak, but nodded and meekly responded, "yah." They continued to eat their supper in silence.

LAST GOODBYE

Isaac jumped off the truck and said bye to his Dad. He turned to David, buckled the seatbelt then teased him, "buckle your seatbelt little boy." David just laughed and pushed him away. They were best of friends. The door closed. Johnny looked at his son, Isaac, and admired the friendship he had developed with David. Johnny had a warm fuzzy feeling and wanted to say, "I love you son", but refrained so not to give David an opportunity to tease his son. That did not last long, as Isaac turned his head, Johnny said, "I love you, son." Isaac turned, waved, and said, "I love you, Dad," but with his back to the truck so David would not hear him as Isaac's legs made a dash to his grandpa's house.

David noticed Grandpa John, standing at the porch steps as the truck sped away tossing dirt and rocks onto the edge of the lawn. David hesitantly waved at Isaac's Grandpa, because he was not sure if Grandpa was waving at him or his Coach. His hand half raised, then turned to look at Coach and he was waving as well. He knew

Grandpa's wave was for both, so he lifted his arm with more enthusiasm and waved back. David turned to Johnny and said, "I'm really tired Coach." Johnny liked being called Coach. It provided an added sense of respect and responsibility.

David's body settled into the seat and Johnny noticed his eye lids half closed before they reached Manning Avenue. The truck slowed and came to the intersection and stopped. Johnny glanced at the rearview mirror, turned his head to the left, then to the right and saw no cars. He decided to watch David's little body take a few deep breaths as he fell into a deep sleep. Johnny looked to the left again and the white fence around the pasture at the corner house with silhouette horses grazing beneath the streaming orange-red clouds was a vision he wanted to keep forever. Johnny slowly accelerated and turned onto Manning Avenue, so not to wake his starting pitcher.

ANXIOUS MOMENTS

ERIE SILENCE AT THE DINING TABLE AS THEY WAITED FOR Johnny's truck to drive onto the dirt driveway. His dinner became cold. His mother, Linda, placed the food back into the pot so it would stay warm until her son arrived. Linda was perplexed and stared at Grandpa, they both understood that it was far too long for their son not to have returned. John lifted himself off the chair and decided to sit and watch the evening news. Isaac followed, but he wanted to sit on the steps outside the porch and wait for his Dad. Isaac sat on the outdoor cement steps and held his breath. He was attempting to listen for the engine noise his Dad's truck would make as it would approach the house, then from behind the screen door; Grandpa interrupted his unconscious meditating by asking if he knew where David lived. "Does he live far?" continued Grandpa. "No, he lives by Tía *Maria's house*," Isaac called out the answer. Then silence again. Isaac lifted himself off the stairs, walked to the living room and sat on the couch to watch the news in the family room as the late afternoon became evening. In the faint distance, Isaac heard a siren. His head lifted and his anxiety increased as he focused his attention on the sound.

He was not alone on the faraway scream of the emergency vehicle. Grandpa had become the guardian of silence facing the emptiness of the night behind the screen door with his ear tuned to the sound. Quickly, Grandpa's parental instincts kicked in. He walked back to the television, grabbed his keys from the desk beside the television and refocused his attention to the area from which the siren's whistle came from. His heart began to pound. Dreadful thoughts screamed in his mind. His focus on the siren made him believe the sound was in the vicinity of his sister Maria's farm which is the area that his son Johnny was driving to drop off David. The siren stopped screaming. Grandpa was confused and anxiously gripped his chest. Linda approached him and without a word they both knew what Grandpa was about to do.

UNKNOWN JOURNEY

J OHN MADE HIS WAY DOWN THE ENTRY STAIRS TO HIS yellow Silverado truck. The engine roared as it reversed, the tires threw dirt and rocks to the rear as it sped onto the road towards the sound of the siren. John looked to his left as he drove east on Englehart toward Manning Avenue and noticed the sun had settled into the horizon, with diminishing sun light, John turned on his head lamps. A few sun rays colored the clouds with orange-red plumes, bewildering the eyesight. He passed his brother-in-law's house near the intersection of Manning Avenue and Englehart when he felt his heart take a few extra heartbeats. He stopped and turned his head to the left and saw no cars. He began to steer his wheel to the right but hesitated and recalled his near-death experience from a car accident. His mind kept retrieving this memory and he could not stop the images from invading his thoughts.

His large yellow Silverado truck quickly spun its tires onto Manning Avenue and headed toward Alta. His truck was moving at a fast rate of speed, when he lifted his foot off the accelerator and asked himself, "what am I doing?"

He had a strange sense of urgency, but he was denying his own gut feeling and slowed his truck to a reasonable speed. However, not knowing made the drive a living nightmare. He reached the intersection of Alta and Manning turned left to his sister's farm. Once again, the truck proved its engine power and within seconds, John was able to see the stop sign at the intersection on Alta and Parlier Avenue. He lifted his foot off the accelerator. He began to tear up, thinking that something may have happened to his son. John shook his head to recover his wits and continued to the next intersection on South and Alta. Finally, he reached the intersection.

His mind kept retrieving the memory when he broke his neck and anguished about the images coming to his mind, then froze for a moment, because of the mental pain created by the past and the unknown status of his son. Time stood still. Again, he shook his head, but violently this time, to stop the memories and take control of himself. It worked. No sooner had he regained his normal state of mind, then a screaming ambulance burst through the four-way intersection and a Sherriff's car nearly hit his car.

He slammed the brake pedal. The car jerked and stopped abruptly as the blur of the Sheriff's car crossed the intersection. This certainly woke him from his nightmarish daydream. He had driven off the side of the road without knowing. With added caution, John checked for other vehicles, as he slipped back onto the road. John could see emergency red and blue lights flickering ahead, just beyond the intersection of South and Alta Avenue. His heart was dreading the unknown, but his curiosity kept him moving toward the emergency lights. The sun hiding behind the horizon and his headlights were not much help in this lonely country road. He accelerated for a moment, then noticed a Sheriff monitoring the cars nearing the accident to slow down and keep moving.

Grandpa slowed down and noticed several cars had stopped to help a person lying on the ground near a vehicle. As he drove by the caution tape; he noticed something familiar about the broken auto. The color was similar, but the door was off to the side of the road, which immediately made him panic. Instinctively, he slowed to a crawl. One of the officers walked up to him and asked John to continue moving. John gazed more intently at the vehicle on its side and said to the officer, "Wait I think that's my truck." "Sir, then please move off to the side of the road," requested the Sheriff. John maneuvered his big yellow Silverado to the side of the road and began to pray that this was not real, because the wreckage he witnessed was terrifying. Now that he was in a state of denial, he also convinced himself that the mangled vehicle was not his. He decided to look again at the wreckage, he stopped breathing, closed his eyes to regain control of his consciousness.

John opened his eyes slowly. He looked to the night sky and slowly brought his vision and focus to the area. "No, God!" he screamed, causing the barking dogs to stop. He knew the truck on its side was his and noticed a group of emergency medics working frantically on someone. He walked slowly, praying, hoping, begging that it was all a mistake and the truck which looked like the one his son was using belonged to someone else. John began to hyperventilate as he got closer to the site. The Sheriff noticed his desperation and walked with him toward the site. "Sir, do you know who this is?" asked the Sheriff. John's crying voice trembled, with tears streaming down his cheeks, "Yes, yes, that's my Son." Sheriff Richardson stopped, held his breath, and placed his arm around John's shoulder and with the most empathetic voice the Sheriff could find, he said, "I am so sorry Sir, could I please see some identification?"

Without looking at the officer, John reached into his back pocket and handed over his driver license. Hands trembling, a soft sobbing voice said, "Here." The Sheriff pulled the flashlight up to the document and looked at the name and compared it to the document he had in his hand. Sheriff Richardson knew this routine too well and dreaded this part of his protocol the most. What and how to say words that invoke painful agony is never easy. He knew now, the person involved in the accident, was the son. "John, I am so sorry, your Son is seriously injured," said the officer in a voice loud enough for John to hear over the sound of the helicopter blades. The emergency team had finished strapping Johnny to the hard board and was ready to place him on the helicopter. "Let me see my Son," demanded John. "Mr. Sanchez, it is better that you meet him at the hospital, he is sedated," requested the officer. "Please go to the hospital," pleaded the officer as the emergency helicopter lifted into the sky and began its journey.

THE WAIT

GRANDMA: LINDA, HAD BECOME TOO SILENT FOR ISAAC. She would always be cleaning, preparing a meal, asking questions about baseball practice or game. Her life's mission was her children and grandchildren. She would not let issues unrelated to her family make her lose her focus. However, Isaac detected a different feeling from her. Her silence was troublesome. Isaac wanted to hold his breath so not to disrupt the silence that surrounded his Grandma.

She was washing dishes at the sink and looking into the darkness through the kitchen window. There was no thought in washing the dishes. She would not look at the sink. The dish was picked up, washed, rinsed, and placed on the dish rack. Automatic response to washing every dirty dish. Suddenly, she stopped and looked at the plate she was about to wash. It was her son's. She lifted the plate to her eyes and her son's leftovers. Isaac noticed her back inhaling and exhaling quickly as if she was taking rapid breaths. He took two steps to her but stopped when he saw her shoulders shaking. Isaac stepped back, but he too was conflicted and needed to be with his Grandma. He was determined to find out what bothered her. Slowly and carefully, Isaac came up from behind her and heard some murmuring.

This was not a good sign. She would pray with a murmuring voice when someone was sick or something serious had occurred. Her eyes focused on her son's house and hoping to see the headlights from her son's vehicle drive onto his driveway. Isaac took a hard step behind her, so to distract her from the trance. He would always push her aside and help her wash dishes after dinner. This time was different. Isaac was scared to approach her. He did not know what to do. He wanted her attention, however he feared breaking the silence. I will touch her shoulder, he thought, but was concerned about her reaction. Grandma always gave him a sense of tranquility, "Yes, Isaac," in a calm and gentle voice, asked Grandma. A sad, but warm voice that allowed Isaac to be free of the tension in the room. "Grandma are you ok?" asked Isaac, as she washed her hands and dried the dishes. "Yes. I am just a little worried about your Grandpa and your Dad," she told Isaac. "Wash your hands".

"I am sure your Dad needed to shop after he dropped off David," uttering her inner hopes. "No, he didn't tell me he was going to the store," responded Isaac with bewilderment. This caused Linda to become more concerned, because her son was very responsible and would always let Isaac know where he was or where he was going. "He said he would be right back, as soon as he dropped of David," declared Isaac. Isaac had confirmed the reason for Grandma's fear and her son Johnny was not home. "Grandma, what are you thinking?" asked Isaac. Just then the phone rang and distracted everyone's state of mind.

It did not ring twice. This phone call was expected. Grandma's eyes flushed with tears as she placed the phone to her face. Isaac noticed and ran up to her with arms embracing her as she grabbed the phone and said, "Hello." An eternity passed after Grandma's first painful sobbing, "No!" Isaac felt tear drops hitting his head and looked up. Grandma's eyes burst with tears. He knew that Grandpa's message was not good, as he read the caller ID on the phone.

THE RIDE HOME

BING! THE ALUMINUM BAT SMASHED THE BALL. DAVID ran as fast as he could to first base. He saw the shortstop move in the direction of the ball. David's legs panicked wanting to be faster than the ball. His lungs took in large gulps of air, then his eyes focused on the white base just feet away, when he noticed a white blur coming straight at him. His left leg reached to touch the bag, as he fell with a throbbing pain on his head, to the side of first base. Darkness and emptiness engulfed his senses. Excruciating pain woke him.

His nose was bleeding. The seat belt securing David's body broke. David began to scream and cry, "Coach, Coach, where are you?" The truck turned on its side after tumbling several times. Windows shattered and David looked to where his coach was sitting but saw only darkness and bright stars. He stopped crying. David was all alone except for the barking dogs at the farmhouses; there was complete silence. He began to panic and hyperventilate, but his instinct to survive took control as he scrambled to exit the truck. He used his legs to climb the door frame, then tumbled to the dirt. David, quickly lifted himself, now head to toe with dirt, oil, tears, and blood. He looked in different directions to orientate himself, then ran to the end of the orchard. He stopped running, quickly turned to where the truck laid on its side. Through the darkness he could see the shadow of a figure laying several yards from the truck.

"Coach?" David whispered to himself. The small truck was on its side. It never crossed his mind that he was hurt, he knew it was critical to get help. His legs wobbled for a few yards and fell to his knees. David wanted to look again. He knew it was his Coach. He had to be brave and started walking toward him. His mind was numb, but his heart told him to help. David continued to move slowly, frightened, but fixated and determined to help his Coach. His Coach moved, then raised his left arm and waved his hand in a gesture for David to go. He stopped, wanting to cry and scream, but his angst was to help his Coach. He continued his mission to the Coach, but again the arm lifted and waved David away. David took two steps back, Coach's arm dropped and became still, which frightened David. He did not know what to do, but his home was just around the corner, so he turned and commanded his legs to run home.

He turned away from Coach, not to abandon him, but to save him. David's legs became the white blur his dream had envisioned. His lungs gasping for oxygen, which gave him more energy and before he could think of being tired, he saw his front door. His hand reached for the doorknob as he noticed his torn shirt and dried blood on his clothes. Strong fingers turned the doorknob and the door flung open, David; out of breath, but not determination, yelled as loud as he could, "Dad help!"

COLLATERAL DAMAGE

DAVID'S MOTHER, ESTELLA, WAS TERRIFYINGLY STARTLED and yelled at her husband, "Michael, come quickly!" David stood at the door gasping for breath, his body covered with dried blood, dirt, and oil, with cheeks streaked by the tears pouring down his face. Michael reached for David, as he fainted from stress and exhaustion. "David, what happened?" commanded Michael. "Dad; Coach, his truck flipped, he's hurt bad, help him!" sobbed David.

David's fragile body shaking uncontrollably. "David! Where is he?" pleaded Michael. "He's by his aunt's house," whispered David. Michael knew exactly where that was located. Reedley is a small town, where everyone knows who you are, therefore Michael knew where his son was referring to. David was placed on the sofa. His mother was dialing for the emergency operator, then looked at her husband, waved and said, "go quickly." Michael swooped the keys from the dish by the door and as he stepped out his thoughts leaned back to his son.

He could hear the loud sobbing from his son and his

heart took a second thought, but his wife looked at him and pointed to the outside as she answered the operator. "Yes, my son has been in an accident," were the last words Michael heard as he left. He was confident that his son would be fine and his mother; being a nurse, would manage that matter. He reached into his pocket, pulled out the car keys, entered the car and tried to insert the key into the ignition; he noticed his hand shaking. He was not tired, or hurt, but the thought of the incident that his son had just experienced made him appreciate his son's courage. The engine roared and the car quickly left Summer Avenue and right onto Alta.

Michael would never have thought the sirens he had heard moments ago would become a chapter in his family's life. He reached the intersection of Summer Avenue and Alta, turned, and noticed from a distance several emergency vehicles with lights flashing and a helicopter flying away from the area. The muffled sound of the rotors made him uncomfortable. Helicopters are not used unless it's a serious situation, and his insight was based on his son's desperate pleading to help his Coach. Michael approached the area slowly, not wanting to disrupt the coordination by the emergency personnel, but he needed to make them aware that his son was involved. A Sheriff, consoling someone, who appeared familiar, but his back was to Michael, looked straight at Michael and raised his hand, in the form of a command to stop, he stopped.

Another officer approached the car as the cool air stirred the sound of the barking dogs. Sirens and conversations from the small crowd gathering on the side of the road stifled the thought process. A flashlight blinded Michaels' eyes and a Sheriff directed him to turn his car around. The officers' voice was firm and direct. Michael looked at the blinding light and behind the silhouette figure he could see the mangled truck from which his son had escaped. "Sir, I think I know that man," pointing to John. "Yes, we all know each other here," responded the officer in a sarcastic tone. Michael held his breath and in a slow and deliberate tone said, "my Son was in this accident," with a firm as a matter-of-fact voice, responded Michael.

"I'm sorry Sir, there are too many things going on, where is your Son and is he OK?," requested the officer. As if on cue, the emergency operator notified the officer to respond to a call from a victim of the accident. "That's my son, he's ok," said Michael. "Sorry sir, I need to attend to your son's call," responded the Sheriff. The Sheriff walked away quickly to his car and drove to Michaels' house. The departure by the Sheriff allowed Michael to park his car on the side of the road behind the other spectators and to notice a man being comforted by another officer.

Michael walked slowly toward the Sheriff and the man, but stopped as he recognized it was the Coach's father, John. As he neared John he heard the officer repeat,

"I'm so sorry, Sir," repeatedly. The helicopter rotors went silent, and the officer let go of John to address Michael. This made John turn and look straight at Michael. He knew that Michaels's son was in the car. John's face became anguished, and a strange feeling of heartbreak came through his eyes. John rushed to Michael, sobbing with a pleading, hoping voice not to hear more shocking news, John asked, "Where is David?" Michael unable to keep from crying as he conveyed that David was ok and being cared for by his mom. A great burden lifted from John. Now he cried only for his son. "He got a bloody nose," continued the conversation.

Michael knew that his son's injuries were insignificant to his son's Coach. He continued his effort to comfort John, along with the Sheriff, but neither had ever experienced losing a child. Their persistence paid off as the tension emanating from the situation began to lessen. Officer Richardson noticed the relationship between John and Michael and asked for Michael's identification. His driver's license was quickly handed to the officer and Michael said, "my son was in the truck with his son," pointing to the up-side-down vehicle. Quickly, the officer removed his hand from John's shoulder and asked Michael if his son was ok. Michael acknowledged the Officer's discomfort and reassured the officer that his son was fine in his mother's care and to notify the other officer that took the emergency call minutes earlier.

A small group of family members that lived nearby approached the two sobbing men and joined in the grief. They began to pray and offer words of encouragement as the night settled and darkness encompassed the gathering. Several officers joined, but they began instructing people to move their vehicles off to the side of the road. Time had stopped. Every motion took an eternity. A tow truck was on site. It slowly moved to the side of the orchard where the truck was on its side and the driver jumped off and pushed the small truck onto its four tires. The tow truck hoisted the mangled vehicle onto the bed and left the scene. This appeared to have ended the immediate morning. Some neighbors and relatives gave John a hug and expressed their condolences as they began their walk to their cars. Within minutes John and his sister Maria were left at the hauntingly quiet scene and a meteor grazed the upper atmosphere leaving a bright shiny trail of light as if to say goodbye. Eyes tearing, hugs shared, emotions shaken and lives altered as the street cleared and traffic returned to a normal flow of a lonely country road.

SUMMARY

A Marine's Peace created from bits and pieces of information from the Marine's real-life journey and family stories of his struggles. John Sanchez, Jr. a Marine Corporal born November 6, 1971, raised in Reedley, California until May 14, 2007, served with honor in the US Marine Corps. The Marine's experiences demonstrated extraordinary valor in the heat of battle and compassion during certain death situations for the enemy. The stories change from present to past as do the nightmares of the Marine. The struggle for mental peace is clearly a challenge as manifested when working on the tractor and his son's baseball practice. He felt betrayed when a young Marine took his last breath and he discovered that media members assisted in informing, preparing, and setting IED's that were responsible for the death of his troops. Vengeance was not the Marine Corporal's way, however executing orders that satisfied that objective, allowed the Marine to free his sense of loss.

The most perplexing emotional moment occurs when the father discovers that his son is being treated by emergency personnel and he is not allowed to go to his side. No moment is more emotionally challenging than seeing your child at death's calling and you cannot stop it from happening. The courage and sentiment of the Marine's mother and the passenger in the truck are breathtaking. Anxiously waiting for headlights to blanket the kitchen window, but instead the Marine's mother received a phone call notifying her of the death of her son and her grandson holding onto her and pleading for news about his father. Quick intense breathing and crying is hard to avert as you experience the tragic emotional abyss from which recovery is impossible. A quick and easy read, but tissues will be necessary.

Printed in the United States
by Baker & Taylor Publisher Services